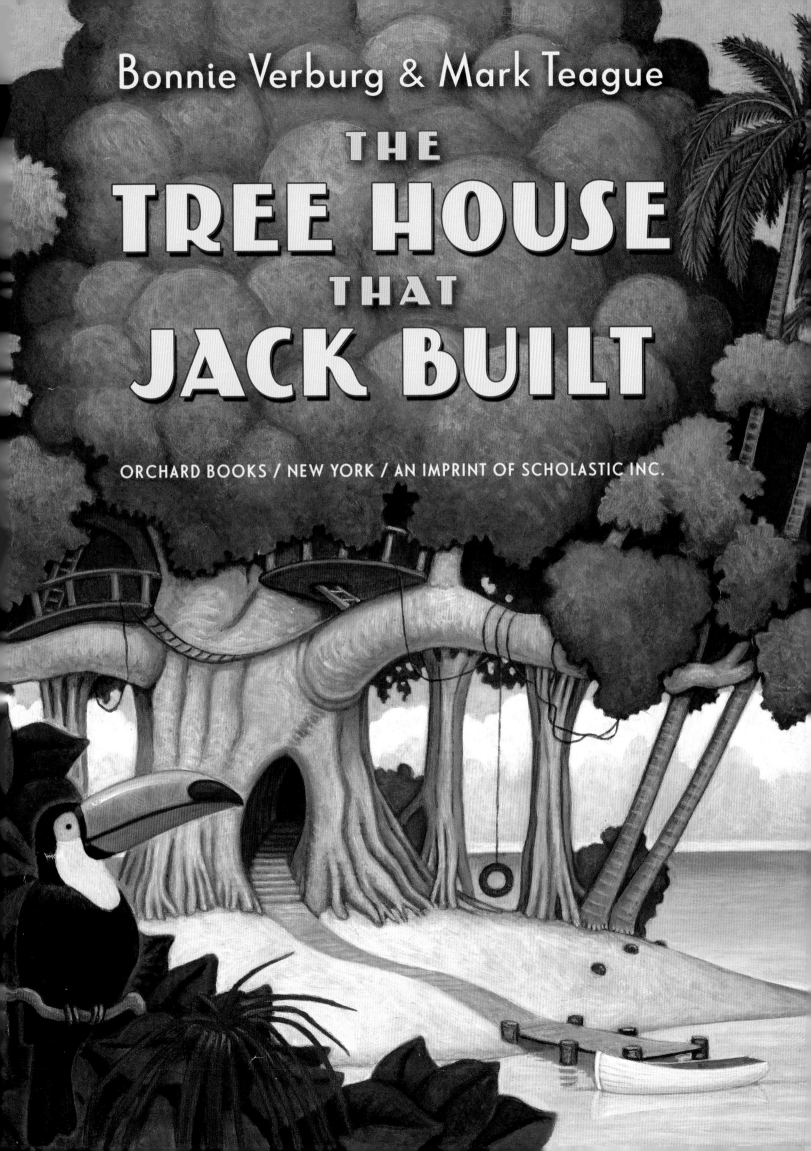

Bonnie Verburg & Mark Teague

THE TREE HOUSE THAT JACK BUILT

ORCHARD BOOKS / NEW YORK / AN IMPRINT OF SCHOLASTIC INC.

The author wishes to thank Audrey & Don Wood, Mark Teague,
Dianne Hess, and Jimmy Buffett, treasured friends
who understand the wonders of a banyan tree.

Library of Congress catalog card number: 2013031121
ISBN 978-0-439-85338-5

10 9 8 7 6 5 4 3 2 1   14 15 16 17 18

Printed in Malaysia   108
Reinforced Binding for Library Use
First edition, June 2014

The display type was set in Le Havre and PAG Bankas.
The text was set in BadgerRR Medium.
The illustrations are acrylic paintings.
Book design by Kathleen Westray

For Robert Martin with love — B.V.

To Lynn Binder — M.T.

HERE IS THE BOY
up in the tree
where he built a house
overlooking the sea.

Yes, this is the tree house
that Jack built.

Here is the fly
that buzzes by
the tree house
that Jack built.

Here is the lizard
that snaps at the fly
that buzzes by
the tree house
that Jack built.

Here is the parrot
who pecks at the lizard
that snaps at the fly
that buzzes by
the tree house
that Jack built.

But who swats the parrot?

Of course it's the cat!

He jumps on the swings,
the ladder, the birdbath,
the marvelous things
Jack made with his tools —
it's a wonder to see
what that clever boy Jack
thought to build in his tree.

And here is the dog
who chases the cat
who swats the parrot
who pecks the lizard
that snaps at the fly
that buzzes by
the tree house
that Jack built.

Here is the snake —
imagine that!

He slides by the dog
who chases the cat.

And here is the monkey
who swings past the snake
on a knotted vine
only Jack could make.

But what is that sound?

Jack's ringing a bell!
It's story time!
They know it well. . . .

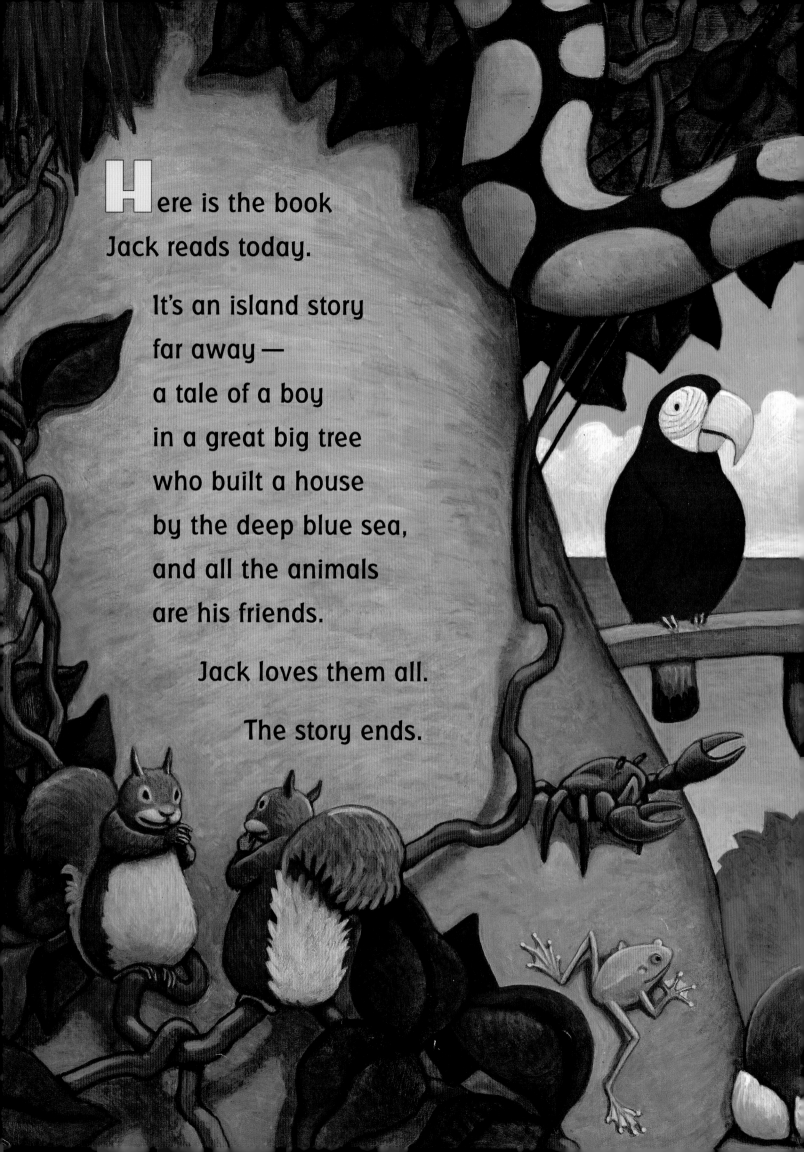

Here is the book
Jack reads today.

It's an island story
far away —
a tale of a boy
in a great big tree
who built a house
by the deep blue sea,
and all the animals
are his friends.

Jack loves them all.

The story ends.

"Read it again!"
they squawk and yell,
but they'll have to wait
for tomorrow's bell
in the tree house
that Jack built.

Now come the whales
swimming one by one,
to leap in the sea
with the setting sun.

And here is the owl
who flies out of the tree
and over the whales
in the darkening sea.

Here are the stars
in the big blue sky
that say good night
when the owl flies by.

Away swim the whales.
The monkey swings home.
The snake slides off,
and the dog has his bone.
The lizard is still.
The bird nods its head.

The tree house is silent
when Jack goes to bed.

The moon has come up.

The night has grown deep.

Now Jack and his kitty
are fast asleep.

Good night to all
who came and played.

Good night to all
the things Jack made.

Good night to the sky.

Good night to the tree.

Good night to you.

Good night to me.

And good night to
the tree house
that Jack built.